Mermaid Indi

Balboa Press books may be ordered through booksellers or by contacting:

Balboa Press
A Division of Hay House
1663 Liberty Drive
Bloomington, IN 47403
www.balboapress.com
1 (877) 407-4847

ISBN: 978-1-5043-1414-5 (sc)
ISBN: 978-1-5043-1415-2 (e)

Print information available on the last page.

Balboa Press rev. date: 07/31/2018

BALBOA

Mermaid Indi

This book is dedicated to Adrian and Indiana. Thank you for your unwavering belief, inspiration and love.

Little mermaid Indi swinging on her
sea swing as happy as can be.

Watching baby fish hatching one, two, three.

She's the guardian of the ocean, a kind and loving friend.

Happy to give a helping hand, to all creatures she will tend.

One day while she was busy, cleaning litter from the sand.

She came across a turtle that was twisted in a band.

As she tried to free the turtle something
caught the corner of her eye.

It was fast and it was big and it made the turtle cry.

"Excuse me mermaid Indi" said the turtle, "Please be quick.

There is a mean shark lurking and I'm an easy pick".

"Hush now darling." said mermaid Indi,
"Don't you worry, don't you cry

I will use my mermaid powers so the shark will not swim by."

As mermaid Indi turned to see the
shark darting here and there.

She noticed that the big mean shark
was covered in some hair.

"Oh see here little turtle." she said with a grin.

"This shark cannot see as he has hair all covering him."

And in a calming voice mermaid Indi quieted the shark.

She quickly took the hair off and she noticed a big mark.

The shark said, "Oh thank you little mermaid. I'm not scary, not at all."

"Some people tried to catch me and they poked me with an oar."

"They started throwing things at me.
Some hair, hats and a ball."

Then the strangest thing happened
and the shark began to bawl.

Mermaid Indi freed the turtle and they
both listened to the shark.

As he told them both of some misconceptions
till it was getting dark.

"Sharks are scary. They are dangerous. Get
out of the water RUN! RUN! RUN!"

"We will eat you, we will harm you, we
might bite you on the bum."

"But we are really not all like that. We can be gentle too."

"And most of us are curious or just as scared of you."

Mermaid Indi and the turtle gave a little knowing nod.

And reassured the shark that they would be part of his squad.

It really doesn't matter what we look like, not a bit.

What's most important is how we act and think.

So, they all set off to spread the word
and help their new friend.

Change perceptions, educate and help amend.

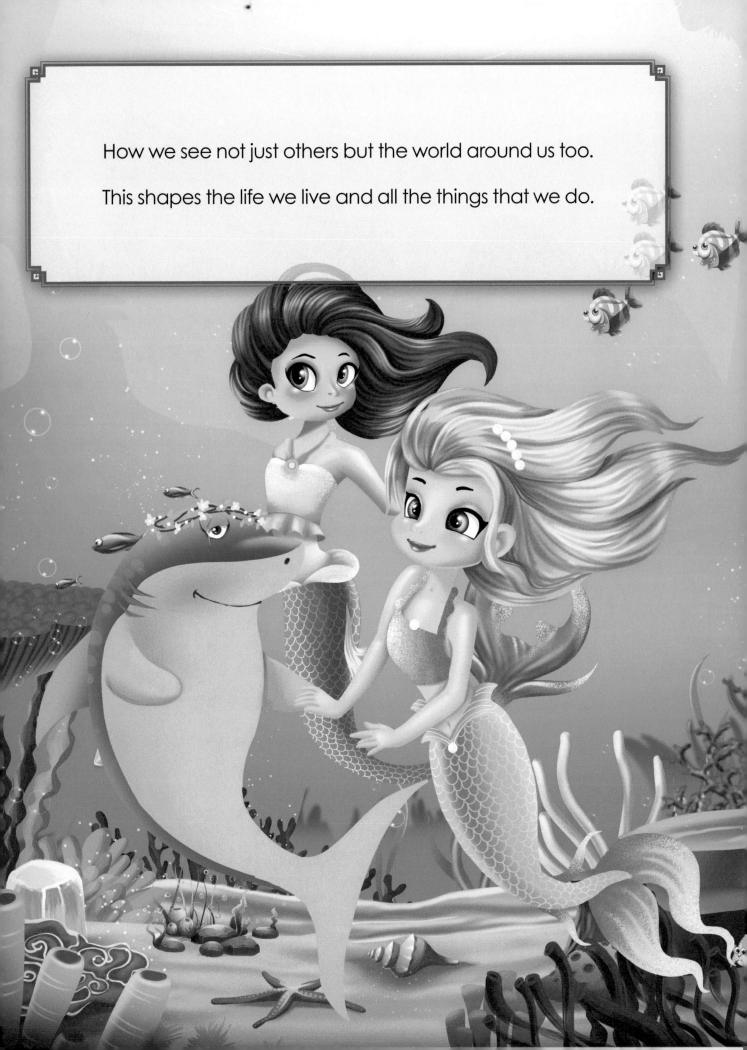

How we see not just others but the world around us too.

This shapes the life we live and all the things that we do.

Sometimes when we see things they are not as they first appear.

And just like mermaid Indi, it's nice if you can hear.

How someone is feeling and what they have been through.

And try to make the day brighter with everything you do.

Printed in the United States
By Bookmasters

ORDERING INFORMATION

Books can be ordered by visiting http://bookstore.westbowpress.com

OR

By mailing checks payable to the author
using order format below:

Betty Pettersen
P.O. Box 14
Lititz, PA 17543

✂ ....

Please send me _____ copies of
AN EAGER CHILD
Growing up in Norway

At $16.95 per book plus $3.00 S & H

Enclosed is my check for $_____

Mail Books To:

_____
Name

_____
Address

_____
City   State   Zip

Contact for further information
Bettty F. Engh Pettersen
abookforyou@hotmail.com